This book belongs to

_____

_____

For Archer & Edi…to celebrate the adventures we have already had and the adventures that are yet to come.

The Magic Easel
To The Beach

By Gem Bridges-Medley

Illustrated by Saskia Fuchs

First published in 2021 by Reach Out Arts UK

ISBN 978-1-7399384-0-6

Children's Book Publishers
A Division of Team Author UK

The Magic Easel

To The Beach

Gem Bridges-Medley

Saskia Fuchs

The bright spring sun shone through the window onto the dining-room table.
"**Are you ready Fritz?**" called Edi as she finished painting at her easel. Fritz knew
what that meant; he ran to her side and wagged his tail so fast you might think
he would take off like a helicopter.

"Come on then boy, let's find out where we are going today."

Fritz woofed in excitement as Edi added the finishing touches to her painting. Edi loved to paint; it was her absolute favourite thing to do.

But, what no one other than Fritz, Edi (and maybe one or two of her friends) knew was that Edi's paintings were magical, so magic in fact that if Edi were to paint an enchanted wonderland it would become so real that they could jump right in! And that's what they did, every afternoon after school.

Edi patted Fritz on the head. **"You know what to do..."** She lifted him up into her arms, tapped the end of her paintbrush into the centre of the painting and counted to three...

"1, 2, 3..." and off they went...shrinking so small that they were now in her painting. But what had Edi painted today? As they headed down the path, Fritz knew exactly where he was; they had been here before.

Seagulls were flying overhead, waves crashing on the sand – it was one of his favourite places to be.

"**The beach!**" they both squealed as they ran towards the water. Fritz was running so fast that his back legs nearly overtook his front legs. "**Fritz…wait up, toes first,**" Edi shouted, but Fritz didn't listen. He jumped straight in….and very quickly jumped straight back out.

"You didn't tell me the sea was cold!" he said.

"Oh, you silly thing," Edi laughed as she wrapped him in a towel.

Brrrrrr!

Shiver!

One big warm cuddle later and Fritz was feeling much better and ready to explore. They discovered caves and rock pools and even built a sandcastle.

After some time exploring, they sat down to rest on the sand dune when
something very colourful caught their eye dancing in the air above the beach.
"What's that, Fritz?" asked Edi.
"I'm not sure, but it sure is a beautiful thing," Fritz said, still wagging his tail.
"A really beautiful thing," Edi nodded.

They noticed a boy
around the same age
as Edi. He was holding
a string that seemed
to be attached to
a beautiful
coloured *thing*.

"Shall we go and
have a look, Fritz?
Maybe that boy can tell
us what it is."

Edi skipped down the sand dune over to the
boy. Fritz decided it would be fun to roll down
the hill. She giggled as Fritz landed at the
bottom and shook the sand from his back.

As they got closer to the boy, they noticed the *thing* had a long beautiful ribbon tail. "Hello, we spotted you from over by the sand dunes, and thought we would come over," Edi explained. "What's your name?"

"Oh hello, I'm AJ! Welcome to the beach." He smiled, then he spotted Fritz and patted him on the head. "I like your dog."

"Thank you. I like your colourful thing," said Fritz.
AJ jumped back in surprise. "You can talk? But you're a dog!"

Thank you!

Fritz strutted in a circle around the boy and announced –
"Of course I can talk; how else am I going to let you know my name?"
"Well, I suppose you wouldn't be able to," replied AJ. "So, what is your name?"
"I'm Fritz," he said proudly, "and this is my best friend, Edi."

"Well, it's nice to meet you both," said AJ as he sent his kite back into the sky.
"What's that you are playing with? It's beautiful," asked Edi.
'That's my kite; I made it myself. Would you like a go?" said AJ.

"Oh yes, please. I've never seen a real kite before, only in pictures. How does it dance like that?" asked Edi.

AJ handed over the strings to Edi. She pulled them gently and watched as the strings made the kite dance in the sky, swirling and twirling, loop de loops and bobbing on the wind. Fritz was enjoying trying to copy the kite's moves by dancing on the sand.

"Wow!" cried Edi. "This is brilliant; I wish I had a kite of my own!"

The boy thought for a moment and replied, "Well, would you like this one?"

"Oh, I couldn't take this one; you spent all that time making it. It's yours, AJ," said Edi.

"I can always make another, you can keep this one," said AJ. "I think Fritz enjoys it too!"

They looked over at Fritz dancing on his two back legs, looking up at the kite that was frolicking in the sky.

"Thank you, AJ, that's really kind of you. We will take care of it, won't we Fritz?" said Edi.

"Of course we will, it's the most wonderful gift we've ever been given," Fritz replied.

AJ smiled, then looked at his watch. "I have to go; my dinner will be ready any minute. Mum will never believe I've met a talking dog," he laughed.
"I hope to see you on the beach again soon."

"You never know," said Edi, giving Fritz a knowing wink.
"Nice to meet you AJ, and thanks for the kite."
"You're welcome," AJ called back loudly as he ran towards the path on the hill.

"Dinner time?" wondered Fritz.

"Already? We haven't been gone that long, have we?" Edi shrugged. "I've had a lovely time at the beach. Have you?"

"A wonderful time indeed," declared a waggy-tailed Fritz.

They both looked out towards the water and with a big wave said, *"Goodbye Sea; Goodbye Sand!"*

Edi tied the kite to Fritz's collar, lifted him up into her arms, pulled her paintbrush from her pocket, closed her eyes and counted to three...
"1, 2, 3!"

When they opened their eyes, they were back in the dining room, beside the easel.

Being back home meant that Fritz couldn't talk anymore but that didn't mean he had forgotten the best part of their adventure.

Fritz looked up at Edi as she opened
the back door wide.

He ran out and darted about the
garden. With a *woosh*, the kite began
to dance above them, swirling and
twirling, loop de loops and bobbing
on the wind. Edi giggled with joy.
Fritz was having the time of his life...

"Come on you two; dinner time! You have been outside all afternoon," called a voice from inside. "I don't know what on earth you both get up to out there for so long!"

DINNER TIME!

"Coming, Mum!" said Edi as she skipped inside with Fritz following behind her.
"I wonder where we should go tomorrow, pup?"

Gem & Saskia are a dynamic duo from Shropshire who have a passion for all things creative, whether live on stage, at an event or in a classroom full of excited imaginations.

"This story is the first of many adventures we hope to take you on. Who knows, we could end up getting in our time machine and having dinner with Henry VIII or jumping into a puddle and sliding down a rainbow into a pot of gold!"

When Gem & Saskia aren't sending Edi and Fritz off on an adventure, they are busy with their creative arts company 'ReachOut Arts'. Whether that is offering creative consultancy support to businesses, providing educational workshops in nursery and school settings or running affordable musical theatre and dance courses for students of all ages, their commitment to providing access to creative, immersive experiences is at the core of everything they do.

For more information about Gem & Saskia and the variety of opportunities offered by ReachOut Arts for events at schools and other settings, please head to:

www.reachoutarts.co.uk

www.medievaldays.com

 @reachoutartsuk

Printed in Great Britain
by Amazon